CAT TALES

True Stories
of Fantastic Felines

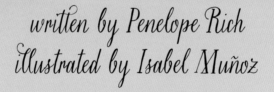

written by Penelope Rich

illustrated by Isabel Muñoz

ARCTURUS

ARCTURUS

This edition published in 2021 by Arcturus Publishing Limited
26/27 Bickels Yard, 151–153 Bermondsey Street,
London SE1 3HA

Copyright © Arcturus Holdings Limited

All rights reserved. No part of this publication may be reproduced,
stored in a retrieval system, or transmitted, in any form or by any means,
electronic, mechanical, photocopying, recording, or otherwise, without
prior written permission in accordance with the provisions of the
Copyright Act 1956 (as amended). Any person or persons who do any
unauthorized act in relation to this publication may be liable to criminal
prosecution and civil claims for damages.

Author: Penelope Rich
Illustrator: Isabel Muñoz
Editors: Stephanie Carey and Donna Gregory
Designer: Allie Oldfield
Art Direction: Rosie Bellwood
Editorial Manager: Joe Harris

ISBN: 978-1-83940-360-6
CH007775NT
Supplier 29, Date 1220, Print run 10472

Printed in China

CONTENTS

Our Relationship with Cats

Cats are the most commonly kept pets in the world. The relationship between people and cats goes back thousands of years, and the more we uncover about our past, the more we see that cats have been living alongside us for longer than we ever knew.

In 2004, a team of French researchers in Cyprus found the remains of a person and a cat buried side by side dating back to more than 9,000 years ago. Cats are not popular in every culture, or with every person. Some people dislike or distrust them, but more of us love them and bring them into our homes and our families. We give them food, shelter, and care in exchange for companionship, affection, and entertainment. A recent study concluded that they actually love us as much as we love them—with the majority of the cats seeking human interaction over food or toys.

There are many cat breeds, all with distinctive looks and characteristics. Siamese are among the smartest, Ragdolls are the most docile, Maine Coons are great hunters, and Sphynxes have lots of playful energy but no fur! Even within each breed, individual cats have their own personality, but they all share common characteristics.

Take their senses, for example. A cat's sense of smell is 14 times better than ours, and their sight is far superior. Their eye shape means they have panoramic vision and they can detect movement much faster. They have excellent night vision, too, and their hearing could be even better than a dog's. These superior senses are the other reason that people of the past took cats into their homes—they are excellent hunters and rid homes of mice, rats, lizards, and snakes. As homes today are more secure, we value their hunting skills less, but appreciate their companionship more.

Many cats are vocal, and almost all of them purr. This purring noise is powerful. It soothes the cat, it soothes its kittens, and it reassures its humans. The combination of their purr, their soft fur, and the way they often seem to enjoy being stroked makes people feel happy, and that's why we love our cats.

Cats Throughout History

What is the difference between a pet cat and a lion? Very little, according to scientists who have studied the DNA in cats going back thousands of years.

Pet cats look exactly like miniature versions of their wild cousins, and they behave in very similar ways. It's hard to train a cat to do something it doesn't already do naturally, but luckily for them, the way small domestic cats like to live happens to fit very well with the way that humans live (and vice versa!). Unlike dogs, who were bred by humans to do specific things, such as hunt, race, protect us, or keep us company, cats seem to have come together with humans more for convenience.

It is likely that the ancestors of today's domestic cat came from both Asia and Africa, populating the Middle East and Egypt. We know much about the ancient Egyptians' love of cats from the tombs and temples that are still standing today.

Our ancesters welcomed these small cats into and around their homes, because they kept them free of mice, rats, and snakes, and it suited the cats to stay for the free food, shelter, and affection. The Romans kept cats, too, as did other ancient civilizations.

As people started to travel on ships to trade, explore, or make war, they took cats with them to protect their food stores. Some cats would jump ship when they reached land, and so cats populated the world in the same way as humans did.

We might not have bred cats for specific jobs as we have done for dogs, but humans have selectively bred cats for their looks, which is how we have so many different kinds (or breeds) of cats. Today's cats make wonderful companions, but as cute as they are, they all still have a little wild cat inside.

Tai Miuwette

The cat held an exalted position in ancient Egypt. In the early dynasties, gods and goddesses were depicted in sculptures and hieroglyphs with lion or leopard heads, but in the later dynasties these changed to representations of the domestic cat. Thousands of mummified cats have been found, as well as statues, carvings, and cat cemeteries. Cat skeletons have been found in royal tombs, alongside milk containers and mice for them to take into the afterlife.

The most famous cat of the ancient Egyptians is the beloved pet of Prince Thutmose, brother of the pharaoh Akhenaten, who ruled Egypt more than 3,000 years ago. Sometimes called Tai Miuwette (Little Mewer), sometimes called Ta-Miaut (She Cat), we know how important she was to Thutmose because he had a lidded stone box, called a sarcophagus, made for her when she died. It is covered with intricate hieroglyphs that show her alongside the funeral gods. These were messages to the gods asking them to care for her in the afterlife.

The reasons why cats were so revered by the ancient Egyptians are probably the same reasons why others have loved and cared for them throughout history. Cats protected the food stores from rats and mice, and killed dangerous snakes, but their usefulness is only half the story. Ancient cats surely shared the same attributes that make them such excellent pets today. They are elegant, amusing, and they keep themselves and their homes clean.

We know from ancient Egyptian paintings that cats looked a little more wild than today's cats. They looked more like servals, with short hair, long legs, and light markings, but, other than that, Tai Miuwette would have been as playful and affectionate as a modern cat, so a young Egyptian prince would have enjoyed her company.

Maneki-Neko

Maneki-Neko, the beckoning cat, is a common Japanese figure of a white cat with one paw raised and a gold coin around its neck. It welcomes visitors, customers, and guests in businesses and homes across Japan, and is a symbol of luck, fortune, and happiness. It is also a popular souvenir for tourists and may have been the inspiration behind the popular Hello Kitty character.

No one knows the true origin of Maneki-Neko, but the story that has caught popular imagination is the legend of Gotokuji Temple, in a district of modern-day Tokyo. Back in the seventeenth century, it was a rundown but tranquil temple looked after by a very poor priest. Despite his poverty, the priest would share the little food he had with a white cat who visited him regularly.

One day, an important samurai and lord of Hikone took shelter under a tree in the grounds of the temple during a rainstorm. He saw the white cat beckoning him into the temple. No doubt curious, the samurai went toward the cat and, at that moment, lightning struck the tree and would have surely injured or even killed the samurai if he were still underneath it. Grateful to the cat for saving his life, he became a patron of the temple and gave land to the priest to support its upkeep. This samurai was said to be the head of the Ii family, whose impressive graves can still be seen there.

Over time, the legend of the cat's good deed spread throughout Asia, and the temple is now a popular tourist attraction. People buy Maneki-Neko figurines and leave them in the temple grounds, hoping it will bring them luck and good fortune. If they look closely enough, they can find a small carving of the beckoning cat in the beautiful wooden pagoda, still bringing prosperity to the temple.

Trim

Trim was the loyal cat companion of Captain Matthew Flinders, a British naval officer, who wrote a heartfelt tribute to his dear friend. Trim was born aboard the HMS *Reliance* in 1799, on a journey from the Cape of Good Hope in South Africa to Botany Bay in eastern Australia. He was popular with the crew because he was smart and affectionate, but his energy sometimes got him into trouble. One night he fell overboard and only survived when someone threw a rope for him to climb. The experience turned him into the ideal ship's cat, able to swim, unafraid of the water, and adept at climbing rigging.

When Flinders returned to London, it was clear that Trim didn't suit a domestic life. Trim's actions often worried those looking after him because he didn't fear heights or strangers. He infuriated others because he lacked the grace of other house cats, who have a way of moving without breaking things. Trim broke everything when he was in pursuit of a mouse! No one could be angry with him for long though, because he would rub against them, purring. Flinders took Trim back to sea on board the HMS *Investigator* to circumnavigate and map the coastline of Australia. On their journey, they were shipwrecked on the Great Barrier Reef for two months, where Trim did his best to keep the crew happy.

When they were rescued, Trim chose to follow Flinders on a smaller ship back to England, rather than go with the rest of the crew to China. However, they only made it as far as modern-day Mauritius, where Flinders was imprisoned for spying. Trim stayed with him, but he ventured out more and more until a French lady asked to adopt him for her daughter. Flinders agreed but the five-year-old cat soon disappeared. The lady put up a reward for his safe return, but trusting Trim, who was loved by so many, was never seen again.

Sevastopol Tom

The story of Sevastopol Tom goes back to 1855, when war was raging in the Crimea between Russia and the Ottoman Empire, which was supported by France, Britain, and Sardinia.

Sevastopol was, and still is, a large, important city, and Russian troops were defending it against the French and British armies. Hundreds of thousands of men, horses, and mules were killed over a year-long siege and supplies of food, medicines, and equipment ran very low on both sides.

When the Russians eventually left, French and British soldiers entered the destroyed city, and out of the debris and devastation came a friendly tabby cat stepping forward to greet Lieutenant William Gair, who was part of a regiment tasked with finding supplies. Gair named him Tom and took him back to his officers' quarters, where he became a popular companion to the war-weary troops. Noticing how well fed Tom was compared to those around him, he wondered where Tom was finding food, and decided to follow Tom on his journeys around the city ruins. He discovered that Tom was a good mouse hunter, but, more importantly, he knew where there were hidden food supplies. Gair was able to find and distribute those supplies, so this little cat helped to save many people from starvation, and undoubtedly helped to lift their spirits, too.

When Gair was sent home, he took his new pet on the ship with him. They lived in peace and harmony together for a year, but sadly Tom died. Gair had grown so fond of him that he had his body preserved, which was a popular thing to do in Victorian England. You can see Tom now (or what everyone hopes and believes to be him) in the National Army Museum in London, greeting visitors and still looking very well fed.

Cats of Royal Families, Presidents & Holy Orders

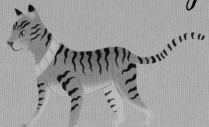

There are well-documented stories about the cats of ancient pharaohs, queens, sultans, and prophets, showing that the cat has held a special place alongside humans for thousands of years.

The ancient Egyptians probably domesticated cats around 4,000 years ago. Tai Miuwette, Prince Tutmose's cat, was only one example of many mummified cats and skeletons found in royal tombs. In tenth-century Japan, cats were so revered that only the nobles could keep them, and in China, too, they were valued pets of the Song dynasty.

According to Islamic lore, the prophet Muhammad loved his cat Muezza so much that he cut off the sleeves of his prayer robe to avoid disturbing Muezza's sleep. Today in Islam, it is a sin to harm a cat.

In Thailand, it is tradition to present a Siamese cat to every new monarch at the coronation. The cat is said to bring warmth and luck to the household—a belief shared by millions around the world. Just as happened with Siam, the first Siamese in the United States, other Thai diplomats gave Siamese cats as gifts to the royal and wealthy, including one called Kotka given to Alexei, son of Russian Czar Nicholas II in 1914.

In the eighteenth century, the Russian empress Elizabeth was given five cats to control the pests at her Winter Palace. They were pampered pets and had their own servants. The palace is now part of the Hermitage Art Museum and many cats still live there today.

In more recent times, Chelsea Clinton's black-and-white cat Socks was popular with photographers as he played in the White House garden, or sat on President Clinton's shoulders, or in his chair in the Oval Office. But these cats, like all cats, seem unimpressed by wealth and power. All they need is for their food bowl to be filled, some love and affection, and a nice warm place to sleep.

Siam

When, in 1879, the US consul in Bangkok in Thailand read in a newspaper that the President's wife loved cats, he decided to send her a gift—the finest example of a Siamese cat that he could find. He named the cat Miss Pussy, and sent her via ship to Hong Kong and then by ocean liner across the Pacific Ocean to San Francisco. It was a very long journey, but Miss Pussy was well looked after by the ship's purser, who knew how precious she was—the first ever Siamese to set paw in the United States. After two months of waiting, First Lady Lucy Rutherford and her children watched excitedly as staff opened the crate, and a beautifully regal cat with mahogany fur looked out at them. They had never seen a cat like it, nor had they probably met one with such an unusual character.

According to legend, Siamese cats guarded ancient temples and were the exclusive pets of the royalty of Siam (modern-day Thailand). Even today's Siamese cats, wherever they live, seem aware of their royal upbringing. They have elegance, poise, and intelligence, and they are naturally curious and playful. So, soon after her arrival, twelve-year-old Fanny Rutherford renamed Miss Pussy "Siam," to give her an appropriately royal name.

Siam quickly adapted to her new home, and although the Rutherfords had two dogs, a goat, and a mockingbird, she became Fanny's special companion. She was free to go where she liked in the White House, and apparently liked to make grand entrances when they had guests.

A year later, when the Rutherfords were away in Ohio, Siam fell ill. The White House staff gave her duck, chicken, fish, and even oysters to try to revive her, but nothing worked. They called the President's doctor, who was a cat-lover, and he took her home to care for her. Sadly she didn't make it, but her memory lives on, as does the popularity of her breed.

Mačak

Mačak was a cat who made an enormous contribution to science. He was the reason that his human friend Nikola Tesla became fascinated with electricity and went on to build one of the most important inventions in modern history.

Nikola Tesla was born in 1856 in the small town of Smilja, then part of Austria but now in modern-day Croatia. Mačak was his best friend and playmate. He called him "the finest of all cats in the world." Wherever Tesla went, Mačak followed and he was fiercely protective. When a person or animal threatened Tesla, Mačak would puff up to double his size, arch his back, raise his tail as straight as an iron bar, and hiss until the culprit backed off. Tesla adored his little black cat and they would play for hours together.

One cold, dry winter's evening, when Tesla was only three, he stroked his friend's back and experienced something that amazed him. Mačak's back was a sheet of light and Tesla's hand produced sparks loud enough to be heard by his family. His father explained that it was "nothing more than electricity," and his mother joked that he should be careful or he may start a fire, causing Tesla's mind to go into overdrive. Later, when it was dark and the candles were lit, Tesla noticed a glowing aura around his cat. This made him wonder about electricity and what it actually was—a question that baffled him till his dying day, despite going on to harness it to the benefit of humankind.

Tesla's brilliant mind never stopped trying to figure out what electricity was, nor how it could be used to create a more efficient motor. After moving to the United States, he eventually invented the induction motor, which improved energy production worldwide. He also played a part in the invention of radio. So, whenever you turn on a light, or an electrical appliance, or see an electric car, be thankful to the young Tesla and his beloved cat Mačak.

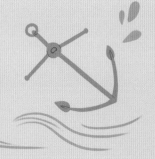

Unsinkable Sam

Unsinkable Sam was the nickname given to a cat who survived the sinking of three warships during World War II. His story demonstrates a kindness to cats during a time when humans were intent on destroying one another. Sam was brought onboard the German warship, *Bismarck*, for its first ever mission in May 1941. He was probably enlisted into the German navy for his hunting abilities, but no doubt was also a popular member of the crew.

After a sea battle that was destructive to both sides, the British navy sunk the *Bismarck*, and of the 2,000 crew, only around 110 men were rescued, and one little black-and-white cat. The British crew of HMS *Cossack* spotted him floating on some wreckage and brought him onboard to safety. He was given the name Oscar, and quickly became accustomed to his new name and surroundings. In October 1941, *Cossack* suffered a direct hit by a German torpedo. Oscar was rescued with the surviving crew. It was at this point that sailors started calling him Unsinkable Sam, but more was to come …

Sam was posted onboard the aircraft carrier HMS *Ark Royal*, which was said to be a lucky ship. A couple of weeks later, it too was hit by a German torpedo. Sam and all but one of the crew were rescued before it sank. Perhaps because of superstition, or perhaps because Sam had been through enough, this marked the end of his naval career. He lived with the Governor of Gibraltar for a while, before being taken to live out his days in Belfast in Northern Ireland. He was at least 14 years old when he died—remarkable, when three of his nine lives were used up in less than a year. It is not clear whether every part of this story is completely true, but Unsinkable Sam was famous—and he remains perhaps the luckiest of unlucky cats.

Simon

In 1949, the British ship HMS *Amethyst* set sail to Nanking from Shanghai in China. On board was a full crew, including Simon and Peggy, the ship's cat and dog. Simon roamed the ship as if it were his own, even sleeping in the Captain's quarters and often enjoying the view from the bridge.

One foggy day in April, they entered the mouth of the Yangtze River and came under attack. A ferocious bombardment of bullets and explosives killed 17 men, including the Captain, and damaged the ship. Simon was found unconscious and badly hurt. The crew took him to a medic, who removed shrapnel from his body and stitched up the wounds. The ship and its crew were stuck in the river for months, in a damaged ship between two armies at war. They repaired the ship, but the attacking army would not let them move, wanting them to surrender. All the while the food was running low and the rats were increasing.

As soon as Simon was well, the new Captain called on him to become the ship's "mouser-in-chief." Simon set to work ridding the ship of its mice and rats to protect the food, and, in doing so, boosted the spirits of the crew. They kept a chart of his successes and celebrated his efforts. It was the one positive thing they had, knowing that guns were pointing at them and food was running low. One dark night, the Captain decided to make a break for safer waters downriver. The ship was fired at, but it wasn't hit and they made it to safety.

Their story spread around the world. When they returned to Britain, Simon received telegrams, parcels of cat food, and the Dickin Medal—awarded to the bravest of animals in the British armed forces—for saving the crew's food and boosting the men's morale. He is the only cat to have received the medal—a real hero.

Faith

This is another story about a brave cat during World War II. Faith was the name given to a plucky stray cat who sought sanctuary in St. Augustine's and St. Faith Church in the City of London. She became a much-loved member of the congregation, and in return for food, shelter, and affection, she kept the mice at bay. In August, the rector noticed she was getting fatter, and one morning, when she didn't turn up for breakfast, Father Ross found her curled up in her basket with a kitten. It was white with black ears and tail, and because of its markings, the little tom was named Panda.

On September 6, Faith pleaded with Father Ross to let her out of his study. She picked up Panda by the scruff of his neck and took him to a cold nook in the basement. Twice, Father Ross gently carried Panda back to the warmth of the basket, but each time Faith took her kitten back down. Realizing that Faith felt that Panda was in some kind of danger, Father Ross brought the basket down and left them snuggling together. Three days later, Father Ross was returning home when the air-raid sirens sounded. He spent the night in a shelter, and woke up to the news that many buildings had been destroyed. St. Augustine's had suffered a direct hit and, a fire officer told him that no one could have survived, not even a cat. Risking his own life, Father Ross searched through the rubble for Faith until he heard a muffled meow. Faith was dusty but uninjured, and underneath her was Panda, safe and sound. Not long after, the church roof collapsed.

The story of Faith's devotion to her kitten spread. She was proposed for a Dickin Medal, but as this was only awarded to animals in the armed forces, Faith was awarded a special silver medal instead—an event that was reported in newspapers worldwide. Father Ross had her photo taken, and his dedication to her began: "Faith ... the bravest cat in the world."

Cats with Jobs

It's strange to think of working cats. All cats are independent and free-roaming creatures, who are difficult to train. It's not because they are less smart than dogs, but perhaps it's because they are unwilling to learn and don't feel the need to please humans as much as dogs do. They don't really care if they are a "good boy."

In this chapter, however, we meet eight cats with jobs. There are those with the most common job for a working cat—ridding buildings and food stores of mice and rats. Towser was a World Champion mouser, employed at a distillery to keep the mice and rats away. Around the world there are animal shelters rehoming feral cats to people who need help with pest control.

Larry was not a feral cat before he became employed as chief mouser at the UK Prime Minister's residence. Feral cats are much better at catching pests than housecats, and Larry was not very good at his job. He had to be moved to a different department and is now a successful ambassador, which is another common job for a cat.

Just like humans, some cats are lucky enough to be at the right place at the right time to land a top job. Take Mayor Stubbs in Alaska, Leon the lawyer in Brazil, and Tama the Station Master. They have no formal duties but they meet and greet visitors and keep people happy.

There are also the photogenic cats who become models or social media stars, the cats who perform on stage or screen, and the cats employed for their super-senses or their perfect temperament.

And then there are the unsung cat heroes around the world, like Pwditat in Wales, who help to comfort and lift the spirits of others. This is the most common "job" that cats have. Do you have one in your home?

Félicette

This is the story of Félicette, a trained astronaut and the first cat in space. In 1963, as the Soviet Union and the United States were competing to be the first to reach the moon, France was developing its own rocket. They started their testing with rats but wanted to try something bigger, so they recruited 14 cats and put them on a strict training regime. Some of the training was the same for the cats as it was for human astronauts, including the G-force centrifuge where they were strapped into a machine and spun round at very high speed.

During each exercise, they monitored the cats' brains, and there was one who remained much calmer than the others—C341, later named Félicette. They gave the cats numbers instead of names so they didn't get too attached to them. Félicette was placed in the nose of a rocket, connected up to monitoring equipment and microphones to check how her body and brain responded to the space flight. The rocket launched at 8.09 a.m. on October 18, 1963, and the flight lasted 13 minutes.

Félicette reached a height of 152 km (94 miles) and experienced zero gravity, and although she was strapped in, it must have felt pretty strange to a cat with no idea what was happening. The nose cone then detached from the rocket, and Félicette returned to Earth by parachute. She was given a large bowl of delicious food for her troubles.

Sadly, all the monitoring caused her to suffer a brain injury a few days later and she was put to sleep. In 2019, a memorial statue of her was unveiled at the International Space University. She is perched on top of the Earth, looking up into the sky, a fitting memorial to a true space pioneer.

Tama

If you live in Japan, you probably know of Tama, the famous station cat. She might even have greeted you when you got off the train at Kishi, because that was Tama's job—and she wore the stationmaster's hat and badge to prove it.

As a kitten, Tama was one of a group of strays who lived near the station. Cats are considered lucky in Japan, so train passengers fed them and fussed over them, but Tama developed a special friendship with local grocer Toshiko Koyama, the informal station manager at the time.

The train company responsible for running the train line was losing money, so it was going to close Kishi station. When locals protested, the company agreed to keep it open, but could not pay people to work there. Instead, Toshiko made Tama the stationmaster, and the company agreed to pay her in cat food.

Word spread quickly, and more and more people arrived in Kishi to meet the adorable new stationmaster. Indeed, Tama proved so popular that, over the next few years, the company made her a special hat, promoted her, appointed two assistants (Tama's mother and sister), and built her a ticket office with built-in litter box. She certainly seemed to be bringing luck to the company, and the wider community.

By 2010, a Tama train, complete with whiskers and Tama cartoons, was bringing people to a newly built station. Tama had become a celebrity!

When she died at the grand old age of 16, the train company gave her a special funeral, attended by 3,000 people. So now, if you go to Kishi station, you will meet Nitama (meaning "second Tama") or one of the young trainees who will proudly wear the stationmaster's hat.

Cat Senses & Sensibilities

Cats are smart and agile, and four of their senses are so superior to ours that cats could be useful in a lot of ways to humans, just as service dogs are. Their smell sensors are far more powerful than ours.

Some researchers even believe a cat's sense of smell is better than a dog's, and that was certainly true of Rusik, who became so good at finding stolen fish in vehicles that he was given the job of chief pet detective over a sniffer dog.

A cat's hearing is also superior to ours, and even better than a dog's at high pitches. This was the key to a special project called Acoustic Kitty launched by the Central Intelligence Agency in the US, to use cats as spies. The theory was that cats could come and go without anyone noticing them, so if a cat got close enough, the CIA could listen in on a conversation. They trained the cats to respond to voice commands given to them through implants in the cats' ears, but what worked in a lab didn't work in reality, as the cats didn't behave as required.

Cats are very sensitive to touch, and their whiskers act as radars and touch receptors. Pwditat used these attributes to act as a "seeing-eye cat" to a blind dog. She rubbed up against him and purred to reassure him, and then she used her receptors and agility to guide him round and open doors for him.

Perhaps a sixth sense comes into play, too, making some cats good at their jobs. Constable Snickers was a much-loved police cat in New Zealand. Her job was to welcome and often soothe the victims of crime who came to the police station.

Lemon was a cat in the Japanese police force who would go with officers to visit victims of scams. They were often vulnerable people who found Lemon a soothing presence. This helped them remember details of the crime more clearly. So as difficult as it is to train cats, there are many out there doing their jobs, using their senses and sensibilities to make a difference.

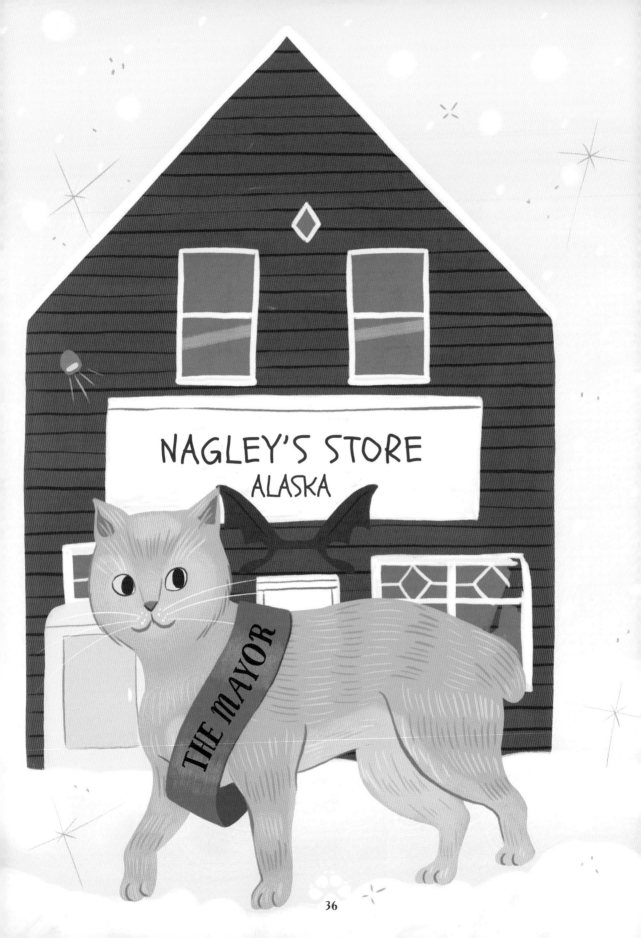

Stubbs

Stubbs lived a long and eventful life. When he was young, he was shot by a BB gun and fell into a fat fryer (not hot, thankfully!). Later, he was voted mayor of his town. And in his old age, he was attacked by a dog and put forward to become a US senator. He died at the grand old age of 20, a life very well lived for a little cat.

Stubbs' rise to fame came when the people of the small town Talkeetna in Alaska wrote his name on the voting paper for mayor. He was a popular member of the community because he lived at Nagley's General Store in the heart of the town, and it is said that the people felt he was more deserving than the human candidates.

The store's general manager had chosen Stubbs from a box full of kittens because Stubbs was unusual—he didn't have a tail, and he was quite a character. Every afternoon he would visit one of the town's restaurants for a drink of catnip, served up in a wine glass.

The story of the cat mayor was great publicity for the town. People visiting Denali (sometimes known as Mount McKinley), the highest mountain in the United States, would stop at the Talkeetna store to visit the mayor. He had many photos taken by tourists, who then shared the story with their friends. Stubbs liked the attention, until he got into an argument with a dog, who hurt Stubbs quite badly.

After that, Stubbs became the face of a new political campaign—not that he knew anything about it. This time he was proposed as a candidate in the US Senate race in Alaska. The thought of a cat sitting on a chair in the Senate is funny, and whoever was behind it was making a political point, but for Stubbs himself he was happy in his comfy basket on the countertop in Nagley's, living his best cat life.

Larry

For almost 100 years, the job of Chief Mouser to the Cabinet Office has been an important role for the government of the United Kingdom. In the past, rats and mice were a real problem in peoples' homes. They would get into food supplies and bring diseases and fleas into the house. Even grand houses had the same problem, so people kept cats to keep the rats and mice away. That included Numbers 10 and 11 Downing Street, where the most important ministers in the UK government live.

In the past, the only requirement was that the cat should be "efficient," but in 2011, when Prime Minister David Cameron took his family to an animal shelter to find his own Chief Mouser, they were looking for a pet for their children, too. They picked a handsome tabby cat called Larry.

The British media loved Larry, and there were many photos of him in the newspapers and online. Larry welcomed visitors, including Presidents Obama and Trump. Larry's profile on the government website said: "Larry spends his days greeting guests to the house, testing antique furniture for napping quality ... and contemplating a solution to the mouse occupancy of the house." What this really means is that Larry was bad at his job—he never caught any mice!

Then a real mouser moved in next door. In 2016, the Chancellor at Number 11 adopted a black-and-white cat called Palmerston. Larry and Palmerston didn't like one another at all, but after a few fights they came to an understanding: Palmerston took over the role of Chief Mouser, and Larry greeted the visitors and provided photo opportunities for the media. Despite a change in the people who live there, Larry and Palmerston worked in Downing Street together until Palmerston's retirement in 2020.

Mr. No Ears

Mr. No Ears was a cat you couldn't miss. He was completely white, with one eye, no ears, and a lot of personality. He was part of a stray community that lived next to a sunny beach in a popular tourist area near Albufiera, Portugal. People who visited the area to enjoy the Portuguese sunshine, beautiful beaches, fabulous food, and warm welcome, would also enjoy meeting this colony of friendly cats. The cats loved the tourists too because they fed them and stroked them, and suddenly Mr. No Ears, the most distinctive of them all, had a following on Facebook.

His Facebook page was run by the charity that looked after the cats. They would take them to the vet, if they needed help, and they would feed them in the winter when the tourists had all gone home. Mr. No Ears became their poster boy and mascot because he was so distinctive.

Then, one day, some people catnapped Mr. No Ears. They said it was because they were worried about him and wanted to look after him, but the charity said it was because he was famous and the couple just wanted to make money. There was a legal battle over him, but before he could be returned to his cat family, poor Mr. No Ears died.

This sad story has a happy ending though. The charity gained lots of supporters, and those supporters donated a huge amount of money to them. This helped the charity to continue to care for the other cats, so Mr. No Ears made a real difference to the lives of his cat family, and he continues to do so to this day.

Leon the Lawyer

During heavy rain, a cute little Siamese kitten decided to take shelter in an office building in Brasília, the capital of Brazil. The office was the headquarters of the Order of Attoneys of Brazil (OAB), an important and very serious institution. Its members didn't usually welcome animals through their doors.

The dilemma for the staff was that this little kitten clearly didn't have a family and had nowhere else to go. What should they do? They could have bundled him up and taken him to an animal shelter, but they decided to let the kitten stay, at least until the rains passed. They gave him a box and fed him.

Unfortunately they started to get complaints about having a stray cat in their reception area. This caused them a problem. Getting complaints from their visitors was not good for the organization, so they did a surprising thing—they gave him an official job as a receptionist. When this was greeted with enthusiasm by their staff and society members, they decided to promote him, and the kitten became Dr. Leon Advogato, cattorney-at-law. They gave him his own door pass, and a very smart tie, so he could greet visitors and attend meetings.

Leon became an Instagram sensation. Now he's a very handsome adult cat with thousands of followers on social media. But the OAB has gone one step farther. They set up a charitable fund to support the organizations that protect stray cats in the area. It's called Instituto Dr. Leon, headed up by the cat himself. One of their first projects was to create feeding stations for strays.

When Leon is not busy with his charity work, he still walks around the building, meeting and greeting people, and playing with toys in the Director's office. He's an amazing ambassador for the organization, and for working cats everywhere.

Rusik

Sniffer dogs are a common sight in airports, and are key members of police and border forces everywhere. They are trained to use their superior sense of smell to sniff out illegal things that people try to smuggle across borders. But have you ever heard of a sniffer cat? Well, this is the story of Rusik, the best fish detective in Russia.

When Rusik was a kitten in 2002, he wandered into a police checkpoint looking for food. The checkpoint was in an area of Russia that borders the Caspian Sea. It was there to stop the illegal theft of sturgeon, an endangered and highly prized fish. Sturgeon eggs are also known as caviar, which is an expensive delicacy and sells for huge sums to top restaurants around the world.

The checkpoint police adopted Rusik and fed him scraps of fish that had been seized from thieves. Because Rusik grew up eating sturgeon, he knew exactly what it smelled like. One day, he jumped into the back of a car and found some stolen fish. After that, he became the police force's secret weapon because he was able to sniff out sturgeon no matter how well it was hidden. In fact, he even took over the sniffer dog's job.

Rusik's death a year later is still unexplained. It is believed by some that he was run over on purpose, for being too good at his job. Perhaps some of the thieves and smugglers wanted to get rid of him. However, Rusik showed the police that cats are ideal partners in the fight against this illegal trade, which is threatening to wipe out the entire sturgeon population in Caspian Sea. It's not common for a cat to be a fish's friend, but maybe it's time for a new team of sniffer cats to take up the fight to save them.

Towser

Towser was a gorgeous fluffy tabby cat who lived and worked at the Glenturret distillery. Glenturret is the oldest whisky distillery in Scotland, dating back to 1775, and Towser was their chief mouser between 1963 and 1987.

Whisky is an alcoholic drink made from grain, and the grain stores were attractive places to hungry mice and birds. The distilleries needed cats to keep the mice at bay, and none were better at their job than Towser. She took her job very seriously, ridding the distillery of 28,899 mice in her long 24 years of employment. This was an average of three mice a day. It is said that she brought each one back to the stillman, the person whose job it was to look after the large metal stills inside which the whisky was made. Who knows what the stillman did with all of those mice!

Towser's extraordinary achievement earned her a place in the Guinness Book of World Records, and up until now, no cat has surpassed her record.

After Towser died, the distillery commissioned a beautiful bronze statue to stand at the entrance, so no one can forget her and the contribution she made. Thirty years later, they also named a whisky after her.

Although Towser was a hard act to follow, the distillery cat tradition continued and Glenturret has kept a cat ever since, as do many distilleries around the world. They are not needed to keep mice out of the grain anymore, but they greet the staff in the morning, welcome visitors, and are adorable ambassadors for the companies.

Pwditat

Dogs and cats are not often known to be the best of friends, but this story from Wales is about an unlikely and touching relationship between a stray cat and a depressed dog with failing eyesight.

Terfel was a chocolate Labrador who was given to Judy Godfrey-Brown by a man who could no longer keep him. After a time, Judy noticed that Terfel's eyesight was getting worse, so she took him to the vet and he was diagnosed with cataracts, a common eye condition that causes the lenses in the eye to cloud over. As his cataracts got worse, Terfel couldn't get used to this hazy new world. He became reserved and spent most of the time curled up on the sofa or in his basket, unwilling to venture out because he could no longer see where he was going. He was a very sad dog, until a stray cat turned up at the house one day, as if she had just decided that Judy's house was going to be her new home. She strolled in, took one look at Terfel, and seemed to know that Terfel needed help. It was the start of a miraculous turnaround in Terfel's outlook on life. The cat started to guide him round, using her paws to open doors for him. Judy called the cat Pwditat, pronounced "Puddy-Tat," and over time the trust between cat and dog grew stronger. Terfel would follow Pwditat into the garden and they even curled up together to sleep.

When Judy became too old to look after them, a friend and cattery owner took them both in. She was amazed by their friendship, especially as Pwditat was a bit of a bully to the other cats, but to Terfel, Pwditat was the best friend a dog could have.

Extraordinary Cats

Cats often do unexpected things. They have finely tuned fight-and-flight responses, which means most of them, except the most docile, will run away when they hear something that scares them, or will hiss or lash out when they feel threatened.

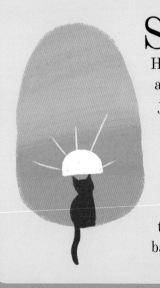

Sometimes, however, there are cats who do the most extraordinary things. Some, like Holly in this chapter, show amazing resilience and a mystical homing instinct. Holly's journey home was 320 km (200 miles), but this is nothing compared to a cat called Jessie in Australia who is said to have journeyed 3,200 km (2,000 miles) back to her old home. Her owners had moved away and they took her with them, leaving their two other cats behind. How Jessie made it back is a mystery.

There are remarkable stories of cats with such strong survival instincts that it makes you believe that a cat really does have nine lives. Just like Unsinkable Sam in the first chapter of this book. In this chapter, we meet Ryzhik, who had to have his paws amputated but managed to adapt to four new titanium paws.

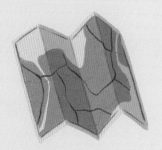

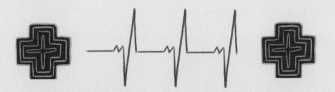

And then there are the amazing parental cats, those who protect children and other animals from harm, such as Masha, Tara, and Gatubela. These stories are so heartwarming that it makes you wonder about a cat's intelligence, and whether they do have a kind of sixth sense that makes them do such surprising and wonderful things. And Toldo, too, showed exceptional loyalty after his beloved owner died.

Every cat has its own personality and some probably do remarkable things that go unnoticed. Others may display an awareness or understanding that people dismiss because they can't believe a cat would be capable of such a thing. After all, what do we really know about the secret life of cats?

Felix

In 1988, the story of Felix the stowaway cat made the newspapers when she flew 288,100 km (179,000 miles) all over the world, hidden in the hold of a Pan-Am plane.

Felix somehow managed to escape from her cage on a flight from Frankfurt in Germany to Los Angeles in the United States. She had been going home with her owners, the Kubecki family, who had been stationed on a US Air Force base in Germany. When her cage arrived empty, they alerted the airline, who went in search of the two-year-old calico cat, but she had disappeared. The Kubeckis thought the worst—either Felix was dead or she'd been stolen, but actually little Felix was playing a very good game of hide and seek.

For the next 29 days the plane continued to fly from Los Angeles to South America, to various countries in Europe, and back again to the States. In total, Felix went on 64 flights, surviving by licking condensation from the plane's walls, but not a whisker was seen of her.

Then, on New Year's Eve, a baggage handler in London saw an animal's tail just as the hold door was closing for takeoff. When the flight returned to London the next day, the crew managed to coax Felix out, thin, weak, and very hungry. A member of the crew offered to look after her until she could go home. They found the Kubeckis' contact details from their lost luggage claim.

Felix spent the next few weeks in quarantine to check she had no illness. Her final flight was very different to the other 64. She returned to Los Angeles in first class, catnapping all the way after a meal of fresh tuna. Her delighted owners were there to greet her, as were many photographers who wanted a photo of this incredible globetrotting cat.

Holly

Holly's story would be remarkable for a dog. For a small tortoiseshell cat, it is nothing short of miraculous. It has mystified her owners and animal experts since 2013 when she returned to her home town after getting lost 320 km (200 miles) away.

The story began when Jacob and Bonnie Richter went on vacation from their home in West Palm Beach in Florida to a rally in Daytona. They were in their motorhome and took Holly with them because she was a home cat, quite used to staying inside. On the last night of the rally, there was a firework display. It spooked Holly so much that she bolted out of the door and ran away.

Heavyhearted, the Richters eventually returned home, but they never lost hope. Holly had a microchip containing her family's contact details, and they hoped that someone in Daytona might find her and get in touch. However, the weeks went by without a call, and the Richters grew sadder and sadder.

Two months later, Barb Mazzola saw a thin tortoiseshell cat sheltering behind her house. It looked sick, so she left out food, eventually building up enough trust to coax the cat inside. Barb took the cat to the vet to be scanned, and the chip told them that her owners lived a mile away. Of course Barb and the vet had no idea that the cat had actually gone missing so far away.

No one will ever know how Holly made it back to West Palm Beach, but she had swollen paws that were rubbed raw, and her claws were worn away. She had probably walked along a road rather than walking across fields or somehow hitching a lift. It might be that she followed a busy highway that runs all the way down Florida's coast, but how she knew where it led is baffling. The Richters were delighted to have her home, and she quickly recovered from her incredible journey.

Germany

Lesvos

Kunkush

In 2016, as civil war raged in Iraq, many Iraqi citizens fled their homeland to find safety in other countries. Many fled with only the things they could carry—the things they needed the most and the things they valued the most. For one mother and her five children, that was their cat, Kunkush, a beautiful white cat with long fur.

The family journeyed overland, and then risked their lives crossing the stretch of water that separates the island of Lesvos in Greece from mainland Turkey. When their small dinghy was pulled up on a landing beach, the desperate people scrambled out of the boat. In the chaos, Kunkush's carrier broke and the terrified cat ran away.

The children and their mother had been through so much, fleeing their home and country, going so far to reach safety, and were incredibly upset to lose Kunkush. After an unsuccessful search, the family had to continue on their journey to a new home. Other countries were helping Greece cope with the thousands of refugees that arrived there, and the family was offered a home in Norway. They were happy to be going to a safe place, but broken-hearted that they had to leave Kunkush behind.

Aid workers who knew about Kunkush found him a few days later in a nearby village. His fur was dirty and matted, and the local strays were bullying him. Knowing how much his family loved him, the aid workers used social media to try to find them. A worldwide community of cat lovers came together and a German lady offered to foster Kunkush because they thought the family had been homed there. After several months of searching, they finally found the family in Norway, and Kunkush made yet another journey to his new home. The tearful reunion was televised around the world as Kunkush's story had touched so many hearts—a happy ending for a family who had been through so much.

Hero Cats

The stories of cats doing heroic things are rare, which makes them all the more astonishing. Having video evidence of those heroic deeds make them irrefutable, such as the video of Tara, who fought off the dog attacking the four-year-old autistic son of her family. She flew at the dog without hesitation and with little concern for her own safety. She rescued the boy from further harm and returned to see if he was okay.

Sammy did a similar thing in Ohio in the United States in 2014. On hearing yelps from Izzy, his dog friend, he ran around to the front of the house and saw the little terrier being attacked by a big, aggressive dog. Sammy puffed up his fur and hissed at the dog enough to distract it, and then he ran with the big dog in pursuit. It gave the family enough time to scoop up and rescue poor little Izzy, while Sammy ran up a tree to safety.

Another cat was hailed a hero when she rescued her five kittens in a fire, getting so badly burned herself that she almost didn't make it. Scarlett kept returning into the fire to pick up her kittens one by one. She touched each one on the nose to check they were all there and alive. She couldn't see them—her eyes were so blistered—but she managed to find them all and bring them to safety.

Some people have reported that their cats have saved their own lives. One cat called Cleo became a UK charity's Hero Cat of the Year in 2014. Her owner became alarmed when Cleo was behaving anxiously, and then found her husband having a heart attack. Cleo stayed with him while paramedics treated him, despite the fact that she was usually scared of strangers. When the husband returned from hospital, Cleo stayed by his side until he recovered.

These stories demonstrate that some cats can be so protective they do heroic things, risking their own safety. Those people who have experienced this first-hand are both grateful and in awe of their cats. Anyone who reads their stories thinks they are awesome, too.

Ryzhik

Siberia is a cold place to live all year round. There is snow on the ground for six months of the year, and temperatures fall to well below freezing in the winter. It is a harsh place for people to live, but for stray cats, it is difficult to survive. Some succumb to frostbite and need to be put down to end their suffering.

Ryzhik chances of survival were slim when he was found in Tomsk in −40 degree temperatures. He had frostbite in all four paws, and gangrene was setting in, but fortunately for Ryzhik, the people who found him wanted to give him a chance at life. They drove him to a skilled veterinarian called Sergey Gorshkov, who agreed that it wasn't Ryzhik's time to die. Instead he created four new titanium paws for him and implanted them in the same way that tooth implants are fixed into the jaw. Ryzhik became the first cat to have four bionic paws.

When Ryzhik woke up from the operation, he had to learn to walk again. It wasn't easy. He had no flexibility in his new paws, so he couldn't jump, but he could walk and get up stairs with a little help, and find a sunny spot in the sunshine to sleep.

The clinic became Ryzhik's new home, and later that year, in July 2019, Gorshkov performed the same operation on another cat called Dymka, who not only had frostbite in her paws, but in her tail and ears as well. This time, Gorshkov had some help. Scientists from the Tomsk Polytechnic University used a 3D printer to create Dymka's new limbs. When Dymka came round from the surgery, she too had to learn to walk again, and she had Ryzhik to show her how it was done.

Dymka now lives with a lady who sends Gorshkov videos of how well she moves. She can run, jump, and play, and is leading a good life, thanks to the skill and kindness of some extraordinary people.

Gatubela

When Diana Lorena Álvarez found her baby son Samuel crawling around the floor in the sitting room of their apartment in Bogota, Columbia, she wondered how in the world he had got out of his cot. Later, when she looked at the babycam to see how he had done it, she couldn't believe her eyes. What amazed her was not how Samuel had climbed out, but how their Siamese cat had saved him from serious injury.

Gatubela was keeping an eye on Samuel from the sofa as he climbed out of the cot. Samuel then crawled over to her to play, talking to her in his own little baby language. After a while, he lost interest and decided to investigate the rest of the room. Samuel headed straight for the door, perhaps to find his mother. She had left the door open after leaving the room, thinking that he was safe in his crib, but there was a very steep staircase right outside the room.

As Samuel got near to the door, Gatubela jumped into action. Quick as a flash, she ran over to him and hopped up onto his back, pawing him until he stopped in his tracks. She then positioned herself in between Samuel and the door, as if making sure he wouldn't attempt an exit again. Samuel sat down and talked some more to the cat, who was flicking her tail, and she then enticed Samuel away from danger. Had the cat not acted when she did, Samuel might have fallen down the stairs and hurt himself badly before his mother returned.

Siamese cats are known for their intelligence, and Gatubela's actions indicate that they might have foresight, too. It was as if she knew what was going to happen if she did nothing. Gatubela means "catwoman" in Spanish and, needless to say, Samuel's parents think she is a real superhero for her intervention that day.

Masha

One cold winter's night in January 2015, Irina Lavrova heard what she thought was an injured cat in the stairwell of her apartment block in the city of Obninsk in Russia. Irina rushed down the stairs to investigate, worried about Masha, the community cat, who lived in a cardboard box at the bottom of the stairwell. She was right to be concerned. The sound was coming from Masha's box, but even though the cat was there, it wasn't Masha making the noise—it was a human baby.

Irina was shocked. What was a baby doing in a stray cat's box in a stairwell? The baby was warmly dressed, and she found a bag of things the baby needed, so Irina, a retired nurse, came to the sad conclusion that the baby's mother had put him there and then abandoned him. She called the emergency services.

When the paramedics arrived, they credited Masha, a large and incredibly fluffy cat, for keeping the baby alive. It seems that Masha got into the box with the sleeping baby and kept him warm for hours before he woke up. If Masha hadn't done that, the subzero temperatures might have caused hypothermia, which is very dangerous for babies.

The paramedics put the baby into the ambulance and were amazed to see that Masha wanted to stay with him. She even followed the ambulance as it pulled away. After tests, it was clear that the baby was fine, and the medical team praised Masha as the real hero that night.

The story went global, and both the baby and Masha received a flood of offers of food, toys, and more from concerned well-wishers. For Masha, though, she was probably just happy that her community showed her a little more love.

Tara

What do we really understand about the bond between a pet cat and its human family? Many think it is cupboard love, meaning they love us because there is food in the cupboard. Maybe a cat just loves the warm, comfortable home and the occasional cuddle. But Tara's bond with her four-year-old buddy Jeremy went one step further when, in 2014, she fought off a dog, saving him from a nasty attack.

Jeremy was out in his driveway playing on his balance bike. His mother was there, too, but didn't notice that the dog next door had managed to get out of the gate. The small dog saw something moving from underneath the car, and its territorial instincts kicked in. He ran round the car, grabbed Jeremy's leg, and dragged him off his bike.

Before Jeremy's mother had even registered what was happening, Tara the cat appeared from nowhere, and leaped at the dog, body-slamming it with her claws extended. The dog had no idea what had hit it, and the shock was enough for it to let go of the boy. Tara then chased it away, hissing and fur bristling, looking very frightening indeed! When the dog ran off, Tara instantly ran back to Jeremy, which shows how protective she felt toward him.

Jeremy had a bite on his leg, which needed some stitches, but otherwise he was okay. The whole incident was caught on the family's CCTV and Jeremy's father uploaded it to YouTube because he thought Tara's actions were extraordinary. Over 25 million people agreed. They watched it, shared it, and TV stations suddenly wanted to meet Tara. She became a celebrity for a while, not only in their hometown of Bakersfield in California but across the United States.

The family will always be grateful to Tara for what she did that day, and the bond between Jeremy and his heroic friend became stronger than ever.

Toldo

It is true that cats behave in strange ways sometimes, but occasionally a cat does something so out of the ordinary that all you can do is shake your head and wonder. And in 2011, in a small village in the Tuscany region of Italy, a cat called Toldo did just that. He took small gifts to his owner's grave every day for two months after he died.

Toldo's relationship with Renzo Iozzelli began when the family adopted him as a kitten from a colony of strays three years before. Toldo grew into a handsome cat, who was always affectionate, especially with Renzo. The family would often find little presents for them at the back door—not the usual presents of small furry animals, but twigs, sticks, toothpicks, and plastic cups. They knew it was Toldo because they saw him doing it.

Sadly, Renzo died. On the day of his funeral, Toldo sniffed at all the flowers, and then followed the coffin and the mourners to the well-kept village cemetery. The next day, his wife and daughter visited the grave and saw a small sprig of acacia on top of it. Renzo's wife knew it was from Toldo, but his daughter dismissed the idea, presuming it was just a sign of her mother's grief. Cats just don't behave that way—do they?

That evening, Renzo's son visited the grave, and found Toldo sitting on top of it. For days afterward, visitors to the cemetery would see Toldo there. Some would chase him away believing animals didn't belong in a cemetery, but Toldo kept returning, sometimes bringing Renzo little gifts as he had done when Renzo was alive.

So maybe the bond between a cat and its human is stronger than some think. That is certainly the case for Toldo and his human best friend.

All Ball

Who knows why All Ball's mother rejected him when he was a four-week-old kitten, but he was lucky to have two very unusual foster mothers. One was a terrier, who took care of him for a short while, and the other was a huge lowland gorilla called Koko.

Koko was born in San Francisco Zoo in the United States in 1971. She spent most of her life being looked after by Penny Patterson, who studied her and taught her English and sign language. It is said that Koko's language ability was the same as a three-year-old child, so she was able to communicate and express herself.

Koko loved the stories of Puss-in-Boots and The Three Little Kittens, and she signed that she wanted a cat. They gave her a lifelike toy to play with, but Koko refused to play with it and signed "sad" repeatedly. So, on her thirteenth birthday, they introduced her to All Ball, still just a fluffy little kitten. They hit it off straight away. Koko gave him his name, probably because she loved to rhyme and he looked like a furry ball.

Koko cared for All Ball as if he were her baby, and All Ball loved to snuggle in Koko's big furry arms. A photo of them appeared on the cover of *National Geographic* magazine and immediately the whole world was in awe of them—two animals that would never have met in the wild showing one another such affection.

As All Ball got older, he started to become more independent, and would wriggle free from Koko's cuddles. Sadly, one day he escaped and ran onto a busy road.

When they told Koko that All Ball had been killed, her carers said it took ten minutes for the information to sink in, and then Koko whimpered and signed, "Sad." Koko had more kittens after All Ball, including a long-term relationship with Smoky, who liked to perch on Koko's head, much to her delight.

Didga

You've probably seen dogs doing amazing tricks, but have you ever seen a skateboarding cat? Well, neither had the people at *Guinness World Records*, until they met Didga in 2016.

They had to travel to the home of Robert Dollwet on the Gold Coast of Australia to meet him, but it was worth the trip. Robert and Didga (short for didgeridoo) put on such a show that they gave them the world record title for "The most tricks performed by a cat in one minute." Didga performed 20 tricks, from sitting and rolling over to a high five and a spin.

The most impressive of all was jumping onto Robert's outstretched palms, two paws on one hand and two paws on the other, and then jumping down onto a skateboard. Robert pushed the skateboard across the room and Didga jumped over a little fence, landing back on the moving skateboard.

So how did Didga learn such tricks? Slowly, according to Robert. It took them a lot of time and dedication. When Robert rescued Didga from a shelter, he could tell she was smart, and she would do anything for some raw kangaroo meat, so Robert decided to train her in the same way as a dog is trained to do tricks. Didga would get a reward every time she did something Robert asked her to do, and this was reinforced over and over again. He would give her treats on the skateboard, and move it a little, which eventually led to her liking the skateboard, and staying onboard.

Robert said that if she didn't want to train, he'd give up and try again another day, because you can't make a cat do anything that it doesn't want to do. Didga's second-best thing (after skateboarding) is sitting next to Robert on the sofa and being petted, when she needs a break from being a superstar.

Famous Cats

If you ask anyone who they think is the most famous cat of all, you'll get different answers from different people, depending on how old they are and where they live in the world. Children and teenagers might say an Instagram cat or a YouTube star, like Grumpy Cat or Maru or whichever cat has the most followers at the time.

There are so many social media stars, all with their own unique look or talent. An older person might know fashion designer Karl Largerfeld's model cat, Choupette, or the three celebrity cats belonging to Taylor Swift. Others might say Bob, the cat who appeared n the book and film *A Street Cat Named Bob*, or they might have heard the stories of astronaut cat Félicette or the millionaire cat Tommaso.

Many cats have a claim to fame—some have a medal for heroism, others have a world record or an award for acting. People bestow all this and more on cats because they hold such a special place in our hearts. They have a charm that many of us can't resist.

As with people, fame is fleeting, and tomorrow a new cat superstar or hero may come along that takes the world by a storm. We might see a cat win a TV talent show for playing the piano, or a hero cat hitting the headlines around the world. There might be a successful spy cat or a cat with a story so amazing that it becomes the subject of a Hollywood blockbuster that smashes box office records.

As unlikely as these events sound, cats never cease to surprise, entertain, and amuse us, so we just don't know what will happen in the future. Watch this space for the next famous cat.

Grumpy Cat

The popularity of cats around the world has never been greater than it is now. Even people without cats seem to love them and the silly things they do. That is why there are so many cat videos on the internet, creating cat celebrities and "petfluencers," animals that help to sell products online. And it all started with Grumpy Cat.

Grumpy Cat, or Tard as her family called her, was the runt of the litter. She was unusually small and had problems with her jaw, which caused her downturned mouth and miserable expression. Tard was a happy cat, she just didn't look it. Tard's rise to internet stardom started when her owner's brother posted a photo of her on the internet in 2012, when she was five months old.

Creative people who saw it turned the photo into gifs and memes, adding words that made the photo even funnier. Like emojis, these gifs of Tard helped people express emotions, such as displeasure, annoyance, irritation, and all things grumpy.

Her owners saw how funny they were, and created an online profile for Tard, giving her the name Grumpy Cat. The rest is history.

Grumpy Cat gathered over 8 million followers on Facebook, and Tard appeared on TV and in a film. She had a waxwork made of her at London's famous Madame Tussauds, and had a range of merchandise from T-shirts to toys. She became even richer when she went to court to fight a case against a coffee company who used her name and likeness on a coffee drink called a "Grumppuccino." She walked away from that with a cool US$750,000 in her cat carrier.

Tard, or Tardar Sauce to give her her full name, died at the age of seven at her home in Phoenix, Arizona, cuddled by her owner. Among those who paid tribute to her was Lil Bub and her other famous feline friends.

Snoopybabe

In 2013, Snoopybabe became a contender for the title of cutest cat on the internet. Hugely popular in his homeland of China with hundreds of thousands of followers on Weibo, Snoopybabe's adorable face soon attracted attention from the world's media. Like Grumpy Cat, he had a downturned mouth, but rather than looking miserable, Snoopybabe's round fluffy face, big brown eyes, and bushy tiger tail made him look like an overgrown lost kitten who needed some love. The online community sent him lots of love in the form of messages and sharing his photos.

Snoopybabe's owner was surprised by the speed at which his popularity grew. She had uploaded the first photos because Snoopybabe was a show-cat. His parents gave him his good looks—one was an American short-haired cat and the other was a Persian, giving him his great big eyes. But what also contributed to Snoopybabe's popularity was the fact that he didn't mind dressing up, so his photos showed him in lots of cute outfits. Of course, Snoopybabe knew very little about his online profile, or his huge number of followers. He was probably just looking into the camera wondering why humans are always so busy, and questioning why they didn't just curl up and have a nice long snooze.

But even at the height of his fame, Snoopybabe couldn't top a Japanese cat called Maru for the top spot of the most-watched cat on the internet. Maru's uniqueness wasn't his looks, but his fondness for jumping into small cardboard boxes. His videos had been watched more than 325 million times in 2016 when he received a Guinness World Record. Even when he was given the certificate, he looked decidedly unimpressed. Like Snoopybabe, he probably wondered what all the fuss was about.

Famous Film Felines

Probably one of the most impressive cat actors was Syn, a Siamese cat who featured in two Disney films, The Incredible Journey in 1963 and That Darn Cat! two years later. Syn co-starred with two dogs, a bear, and a lynx. He seemed to take most of it in his stride and did some impressive stunt work.

The very first cat actor appeared in a short black-and-white film called A Little Hero in 1913. The cat is the villain, trying to get into a birdcage, and the hero is a dog who chases the cat away with the help of some puppy pals. The cat was Pepper, an accidental film star who was born underneath the floorboards of a Hollywood set. When he poked his head up during filming, the director found him so appealing that he adopted him and turned him into a star.

A beautiful Persian cat called Solomon featured in the James Bond film *You Only Live Twice*, as the adored pet of the villain Blofeld. On set, this poor cat was so scared by the explosions that he tried to escape and wet himself all over the actor. He was unharmed, and after a short while was back to performing stunts.

Two white Persians cats, Foster and Fritz, were used to play the role of evil Mr. Tickles in the film *Cats and Dogs*. They starred alongside 31 other cats and 27 dogs. Today, animal welfare is taken very seriously, and CGI animation is used instead of subjecting the cats to explosions and working alongside other animals, or making them do stunts.

The 5th Taiwan Cat Film Festival took place in 2020, celebrating cats for their film roles. And in France, the Palme de Whiskers is an award given for the Best Feline Performance at the famous Cannes Film Festival. It is a tongue-in-cheek award, but it shines a spotlight on all those glamorous cats of the big screen.

Hemingway's Cats

Ernest Hemingway is one of the most famous writers of the twentieth century, and a well known cat-lover. He once wrote: "A cat has absolute emotional honesty: Human beings, for one reason or another, may hide their feelings, but a cat does not." For a time, he lived in a beautiful house in Key West, Florida, surrounded by his children and many cats. These "purr factories," as he called them, amused him and gave him comfort.

The house is now the Ernest Hemingway Museum. They state on their website that Hemingway was given a six-toed cat called Snow White by a ship's captain when Hemingway admired the cat's unusual paws. Other accounts call the cat Snowball, but whatever his name was, it seems that he fathered quite a few kittens, as there are now more than 40 six-toed cats living at the museum, probably all descended from him.

Cats usually have five front toes and four back toes, but polydactyl cats, or mitten cats as they are affectionately called, have six toes. This genetic adaptation makes their paws bigger than other cats' paws. It looks as if they have thumbs. It is said that they make good ship's cats as they can grip the deck better when chasing mice.

When Hemingway moved to Cuba, his collection of cats grew. He wrote in a letter that he didn't really notice how many cats he had until they all moved, like a mass migration, at feeding time. But there was one special cat in Hemingway's life at that time. Boise was a constant companion, who took walks with him at dawn, kept him company as he wrote, and ate dinner with him every evening, sometimes eating off his plate. Hemingway loved his feline friend so much that he devoted thirty-five pages to him in his novel *Islands in the Stream.*

Tommaso

In some countries a black cat is lucky. In others, they are unlucky. But in Italy in 2011, one striking black cat called Tommaso became the luckiest cat in the world. He inherited 10 million euros from his lady owner, becoming one of the richest cats ever. He not only inherited money, but houses, apartments, and land all over Italy.

Tommaso was only four years old when his lady owner died. She was 94, so he had come into her life late, but he clearly gave her a lot of love and pleasure. The lady had inherited her wealth from her father, who was a successful builder, and she had lost her husband when she was quite young. She suffered from loneliness, so she adopted Tommaso, who was a stray on the streets of Rome, and he became her closest living companion. In a handwritten will sent to her lawyers, she left her fortune to Tommaso, asking them to find a charity to look after him. They were unable to find one that gave the lady the assurance she wanted. In the meantime, she met a younger woman in the park who was also a cat-lover. Stefania started to take her own cat on play dates to the old lady's house, and they struck up a friendship. Stefania was a nurse and she started to take care of the old lady, helping her to wash, giving her meals, and helping her to get around.

When the lady died, Stefania said, "I promised her that I would look after the cat when she was no longer around. She wanted to be sure that Tommaso would be loved and cuddled. But I never imagined that she had this sort of wealth." Despite his fortune, Tommaso is not number one on the Pet Rich List. That is Gunther IV, an Alsatian worth around US$375 million. Also on the list is Grumpy Cat, Taylor Swift's cat, and a self-made millionaire bear called Bart.

Choupette

Celebrity, model, Instagram star, and heiress—Choupette lived a life most of us can only dream about. The beautiful Birman cat flew around the world in private jets, ate caviar, and had people to take care of her every need.

Choupette's rise to fame and fortune began when as a little kitten she went to stay with Karl Lagerfeld, a very famous fashion designer, in his apartment in Paris. Her owner, a model, had to go abroad, so he asked Karl to look after her. At first, Karl was not keen because of all the fur in his apartment, but agreed because he knew cats basically looked after themselves. However, when the friend returned and took Choupette home, Karl was so upset he wouldn't talk to him. His friend realized Karl had fallen in love with her, so he gave Choupette back to Karl. He was very moved by this, saying: "No one could give me a more beautiful gift. She has brought sunshine to my life."

Karl took Choupette everywhere with him, and even designed an exclusive cat carrier for her. She ate caviar from silver plates, and on the table, never on the floor. She appeared in fashion magazines, and Karl's fashion collection in 2012 included a shade of blue that was inspired by Choupette's piercing blue eyes.

Choupette became a millionaire, with her own bank account. She had a range of make-up named after her, a book, and a line of merchandise. She was even appointed as an ambassador for a car manufacturer.

When Karl died in 2019, he left some of his fortune to Choupette so she could have the life she was used to. She went to live with Karl's housekeeper, who loved Choupette, but no one could ever love her more than Karl did.

Kedi

Istanbul is a city in Turkey where Europe meets Asia. Traders have been visiting for thousands of years in ships carrying gold, silks, and spices. Some of the ship's cats would jump to shore, and today there is every kind of cat imaginable living on the streets.

Seven of these strays are the stars of a documentary film, *Kedi*, which is Turkish for cat. Two of the cats, Sari and Bengü, are devoted mothers. Sari is a ginger-and-white female who cruises around the cafés and market stalls scrounging food for her kittens. Bengü charms rugged fishermen into feeding her and grooming her. The director mounted a camera on a toy car to follow the cats along the streets and back to their kittens. There are the boss cats, Psikopat and Gamsiz. Psikopat is a fish thief, who bullies her mate and terrorizes the other local cats and dogs. Gamsiz is a tomcat who goes where he likes and does what he likes. He enters people's homes and pesters them until they give him food.

There are the restaurant cats, Aslan and Duman. Aslan is a beautiful cat who turned up one day at a seafront restaurant and started ridding the area of mice in return for food. "We didn't tell him to hunt the mice. He just assumed it as his duty." Duman is a big cat with refined tastes and good manners. He doesn't bother the diners and never enters the restaurant, even if the door is open. He simply stands up and paws on the window for his smoked meat and cheese.

Deniz is a young male who lives in the market and is friends with everyone—cats and humans. He's mischievous and the market traders love him.

The film captured the hearts of people around the world, earning more than US$2.7 million in the US alone. The director, Ceyda Toran, calls it her love letter to the city and its cats, without whom Istanbul would lose part of its soul.

Luigi

Luigi the cat and his best friend Bandito the pug attracted a lot of online attention when their owners took them on a trip all around Spain, and uploaded photos along the way. According to owners Sebastian (Seb) Smetham and Finn Paus, it was Luigi who first decided to jump on a backpack, and perch there like an owl. And whatever Luigi did, Bandito wanted to do the same, so he jumped on too! They spent 46 days together, walking the Camino de Santiago, a network of ancient pilgrim trails across northern Spain. Dog and cat sometimes walked, and sometimes they took it easy in their pet buggy. The four then continued their travels through Spain, feeling safe and happy in one another's company.

In a video, Seb said that the "bromance" between the dog and cat had started back at their apartment in Barcelona, with Bandito showering Luigi with love and licks, and Luigi responding with play fighting and fun. Seb and Finn decided to go on a big trip, but they didn't want to leave the animals behind, so they got them used to the tent and buggy by setting them up in the apartment. First, they took them on day trips before tackling the Camino de Santiago. They settled again in Marbella in southern Spain, and it was here that Bandito became unwell. His breathing changed, so they took him to the vet and got lots of medicine, but sadly Bandito didn't make it through the night. Luigi had lost his best friend, and according to Seb, seemed to show his sadness.

Two days later, they heard that an animal shelter was looking for a home for two five-week-old kittens who had been abandoned. It seemed like fate. They brought the kittens home, and it didn't take long before Luigi was showering them with the love and fun that Bandito had so appreciated. "Within about a week," Seb said, "they were napping together. A new friendship was born."

Bob

Bob is known worldwide as the subject of the popular book and movie *A Street Cat Named Bob*. When the ginger tomcat decided to share his life with a homeless man, James Bowen, the loyalty and love between them was not only extraordinary, it changed both of their lives and their fortunes forever.

James was born in the UK, but moved to Australia when his parents divorced. He was bullied at school and became a bit of a "tearaway," so at 18, he returned to England and started to sleep rough on the streets of London. Ten tough years later, James was offered a temporary place to stay. Every day he went busking, and he started to sell *The Big Issue*, a magazine that enables its homeless sellers to earn money. One evening, James found an injured cat in the stairwell. James asked around, but no one knew the cat, so he gathered the money he had and took it to the vet. The cat was given medicine, so James decided to take care of it until it was better, and then he'd let it go.

The day came, and James went off busking again with his guitar, but when he got to the bus stop, he saw the cat had followed him. Then the cat jumped on the bus. James figured he wanted to tag along, so he took him to his busking spot in Covent Garden and then home again on his shoulders. The next day, James bought him a harness and a knitted scarf, and gave him the name Bob. The days went by and this unlikely couple got lots of admirers. Locals bought the magazine and tourists uploaded pictures and videos to social media.

Soon, a literary agent saw them, and they embarked on a career together. In 2019, they each found a new kind of love. James met Monika and Bob met her tortoiseshell cat Pom Pom, and as with all good stories, they lived happily ever after until Bob sadly died in 2020. James credits Bob with turning his life around.

Caring for Cats and Kittens

Cats are independent creatures that don't need or want too much from their humans, but there are some very important things you should do as a good pet-owner.

Make your kitten feel safe
It's important to provide a safe space to sleep—ideally a soft bed, away from noise and draughts. Your kitten may or may not sleep there, but they need somewhere to go if they're scared.

Training
As soon as you bring a cat or kitten home, show them their litter box. Cats are clean animals and they like to cover up their poop, so they will quickly learn to use it. You must change the litter regularly.

Food
Special kitten food has the nutrients they need to grow into healthy cats. Kittens prefer small meals throughout the day, but cats can have just one or two larger meals.

Exercise
Indoor cats need lots of toys to keep them active. Rotate the toys and play different games to make sure they don't get bored.